MySELF  Bookshelf

Oh That Snow!

By JeongHo Kim

Illustrated by SeoJeong Ok

Language Arts Consultant: Joy Cowley

NORWOOD HOUSE PRESS

Chicago, Illinois

DEAR CAREGIVER

MySELF Bookshelf is a series of books that support children's social emotional learning. SEL has been proven to promote not only the development of self-awareness, responsibility, and positive relationships, but also academic achievement.

Current research reveals that the part of the brain that manages emotion is directly connected to the part of the brain that is used in cognitive tasks, such as: problem solving, logic, reasoning, and critical thinking—all of which are at the heart of learning.

SEL is also directly linked to what are referred to as 21st Century Skills: collaboration, communication, creativity, and critical thinking. MySELF Bookshelf offers an early start that will help children build the competencies for success in school and life.

In these delightful books, young children practice early reading skills while learning how to manage their own feelings and how to be considerate of other perspectives. Each book focuses on aspects of SEL that help children develop social competence that will benefit them in their relationships with others as well as in their school success. The charming characters in the stories model positive traits such as: responsibility, goal setting, determination, patience, and celebrating differences. At the end of each story, you will find a letter that highlights the positive traits and an activity or discussion to help your child apply SEL to his or her own life.

Above all, the most important part of the reading experience is to have fun and enjoy it!

Sincerely,

Shannon Cannon

Shannon Cannon, Ph.D.
Literacy and SEL Consultant

Norwood House Press • P.O. Box 316598 • Chicago, Illinois 60631
For more information about Norwood House Press please visit our website at www.norwoodhousepress.com or call 866-565-2900.

Shannon Cannon – Literacy and SEL Consultant
Joy Cowley – English Language Arts Consultant
Mary Lindeen – Consulting Editor

Paperback ISBN: 978-1-60357-697-0

The Library of Congress has cataloged the original hardcover edition with the following call number: 2014030342

Manufactured in the United States of America in Stevens Point, Wisconsin.
263N—122014

4

Snow was falling in the night.
Tory Rabbit went to the storeroom
to get his sled. He would use it tomorrow!
The thought made his heart beat fast.

The next morning, the earth was white.
Sledding was exciting and so much fun.
Wheeee! Tory's ears got frozen
and his nose turned red from the cold.
But he was playing with his friends
and he didn't care.

6

A young raccoon's sled skidded
in front of Grandmother Fox's house.
"Ow! My Nose!" cried the raccoon.

8

Grandmother Fox came back from town
with her shopping basket.
She slipped in front of the raccoon's house.
"Ow!' she cried. "My arms!"

Grandmother Fox got angry
with Uncle Raccoon.
"You should have cleared the snow!
I slipped and hurt my arms!"

Uncle Raccoon said,
"You should clear your snow!
My nephew skidded and hurt his nose."

Just then, someone yelled, "Watch out!"
A cart rolled down and hit a tree.

Grandfather Bear said, "It's lucky
no one got hurt by that cart.
I slipped on the icy snow and the
handle slipped out of my hand.

Grandfather Bear held a meeting.
"When snow gets hard and icy,
it is dangerous," he said.
"We must clear away the snow
in front of our houses."

The other animals all agreed.

A few days later, it snowed again.
Snow piled up and became icy.
But the only animals that came out
to clear away the snow were
Grandfather Bear and Tory Rabbit.

Dig! Dig! Dig!
Grandfather Bear cleared away snow
in front of the other houses.

"Why are you doing other houses?"
Tory asked.

"Once we make a promise,
we should keep it," was the reply.

"Then I will help too," said Tory
and he swept with his broom.

All the paths were clear
and the snow was piled up
in heaps against the houses.
"Let's do something wonderful,"
Grandfather Bear said to Tory,
and they made a rabbit out of snow.

When the animals came out, they were very surprised.
There were snow animals in front of all of the houses.
The animals apologized to Grandfather Bear.
We're sorry. The next time, we will clear the snow away."

A few days later,
snow fell again over the town.

The animals got up early and got to work.
Everyone cleared away their snow.
Then the children made snow animals.
Everyone had a great day.

Dear Tory Rabbit,

I was so glad that you came out to help me clear away the snow. You are the only other animal that kept his promise to clean up after the next snow. You are only a young rabbit, but you kept your promise when the other grown-ups did not. You should be very proud of yourself.

I know that it was a lot of hard work to clear all that snow, and you were a great help. I don't know if I could have done all of that work without you. You helped all of the other animals and you were a very big help to me.

It's not always fun or easy to keep a promise, but it is an important thing to do. Keeping a promise lets other people know that they can count on you and trust you. It is the sign of a good friend and a good leader. I think you are going to grow up to be a great rabbit, Tory.

Your neighbor,
Grandfather Bear

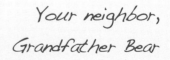

28

SOCIAL AND EMOTIONAL LEARNING FOCUS
Keeping a Promise

Tory Rabbit kept his promise to help clear the snow. Do you keep your promises? When you do, you show others that you are dependable and have integrity. Being dependable means that you do what you say you will do. Having integrity means to know the difference between right and wrong and doing what is right even when it is hard. It also means doing what is right because it is the right thing to do, not for attention or recognition.

You can be a star just like Tory Rabbit. Think of the promises you have made and make a banner to remind you to keep them.

- Use the pattern below to draw a shooting star on a piece of paper or even poster board.
- Write your promises on the "tails."
- Decorate your poster and hang it where you can see it every day.

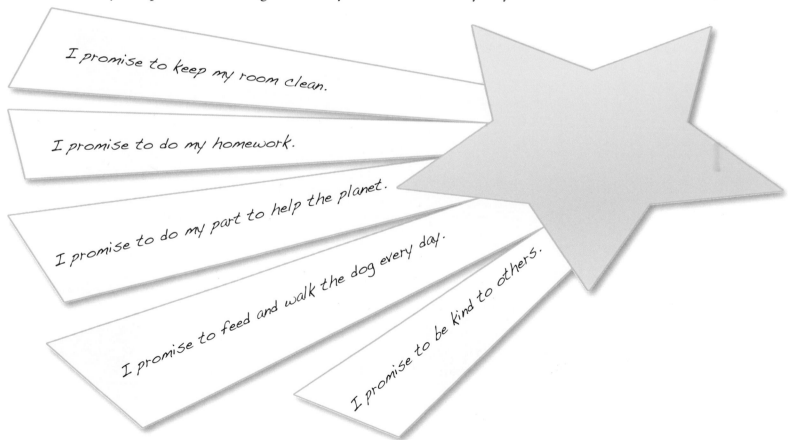

I promise to keep my room clean.

I promise to do my homework.

I promise to do my part to help the planet.

I promise to feed and walk the dog every day.

I promise to be kind to others.

Try this too ... *(continued on next page)*

Here are a few quotes you can write in the star:

"Real integrity is doing the right thing, knowing that nobody's going to know whether you did it or not."   — *Oprah Winfrey*

Integrity has no need of rules.

— *Albert Camus*

Keep every promise you make and only make promises you can keep.

— *Anthony Hitt*

Reader's Theater

Reader's Theater is an interactive approach to reading that allows students to understand each story through dramatic interpretation. By involving students in reading, listening, and speaking activities, they provide an integrated approach for students to develop fluency and comprehension. A Reader's Theater edition of this book is available online. You can access the script by scanning the QR code to the right or visit our website at: http://www.norwoodhousepress.com/ohthatsnow.aspx